A Lesson For Jiggs

For the Young and Old

Murray M Smith

A Lesson For Jiggs is a fictitious story about a legendary cat named Jiggs.

Jiggs was born in the 1920's and lived in several lighthouses along the Northern California Coastline. The story is written to delight the 4-8 year old child. The author has woven into the story a moral issue that can be discussed as the reader sees fit.

Jiggs is a cocky and overbearing cat that is enlightened to his faults. The story uses a messenger to bring Jiggs this enlightenment. Jiggs doesn't realize that the messenger has becomes a part of his conscience as he strives to overcome his shortcomings.

Credits: Thanks to everyone whether they helped or not!

From the Imagination of: Murray M Smith
Artistic Notions by: Jonathon Wilson
Hand Painting: Darice McGuire

Paperback ISBN: 978-1-64718-346-2
Hardcover ISBN: 978-1-64718-347-9

Hello, I am Jiggs. That is, my name is Jiggs, or was Jiggs. You see, I am a cat, or I was a cat. Let me put it this way... in the first of my nine lives, I was a cat.

I had a wonderful life.

My master's name was James.

We lived in the Point Pinos Lighthouse, in Pacific Grove, California.

Let's first set the record straight, I was the MASTER!

James fed me, scratched under my chin, and opened the door
for me whenever I demanded. Of course, I was the master.

Point Pinos Lighthouse, Pacific Grove, California.

My most important job was to remind James when
to turn on the light in the lighthouse.

Ship captains used this light to warn them of the rocky shores.

My other jobs were to catch mice, to meet the mailman, and to carry the mail to James.

My story begins not so long ago.

One spring day, I was napping in our yard and enjoying the warm sunshine.

The next thing I knew, a black crow swooped down on me.

He was cackling like an old hen.

Not again, I thought. The last time a black crow
came here squawking like this, we had the worst
storm in the history of the lighthouse.

I wonder what bad thing the black crow will bring this time?

The black crow was still squawking when I heard
the sound of our front gate opening.

I looked up and saw a strange man walking down our pathway.
He was dressed in a long dark trench coat and wore a hat
with the brim turned down, as if he were expecting rain.

The strange man walked straight to our
front door and rang the doorbell.

I wondered if he was bringing the bad news that I knew was coming.

When James opened the door, I sneaked
quickly through the doorway.

I headed straight for my cradle that James had set up for me next to the pot-bellied stove. I was happy to be rid of that awful black crow and anxious to hear what the strange man had to say.

As he began to speak, I perked up my ears so I didn't miss anything.

"My name is Mr. Featherbee," he said, "and I am from the Maritime Commission. The Commission has decided to close the Point Pinos Lighthouse. Computers are now guiding the ships to miss the rocky shores."

"NO!" I screamed, "You can't do that. The lighthouse is our home."

This was the worst news I had ever heard. Angrily, I jumped from my cradle out through the open window. I realized immediately; however, that I had made a terrible mistake.

I had completely forgotten about the bramble patch that grew last year, and I was headed right for the middle of it.

OUCH! This is going to hurt.

Why do bad things happen at the worst possible time?

After I picked all the stickers out of me, I started looking for the black crow.

He is responsible for this whole mess.

When I find him, I will teach him a thing or two.

By the time I found him, he was sitting on the branch of
a cypress tree watching me. He was so calm I wondered
why he had wasted his time making me so miserable.

Everyone knows that black crows are very wise. Maybe he had a reason to bother me. Perhaps he was only trying to warn me that something bad was going to happen.

But, if that were true, it would mean that I was wrong to blame the black crow.

This whole mess is very confusing, I thought. I have never been wrong.

I was still thinking about this when the black crow
left his perch in the cypress tree, swooped down over
my head and headed out toward the open sea.

Good, he is finally gone. Now I can take a short nap before dinner.

I had just fallen asleep, when the black crow flew back
over my head, and landed so close he frightened me.

He then began telling me I was selfish, and thought only of myself.
He said there was a BIGGER PLAN, and I was not in control. He
continued on, and on, and on, until my head started spinning.

It seemed like hours the black crow continued, until our foghorn interrupted him. HOOOOT! HOOOOT!

The foghorn startled me, as well, and when I looked up I saw that a layer of coastal fog had covered the sun, and the north wind had begun to blow.

I no longer heard the black crow squawking, but I felt he was near. So, I called out, "Black crow, black crow, where are you?" There was no answer, and I didn't see him anywhere. Where had he gone? Did I only dream that he had returned from the sea?

I looked again for the black crow, but he had definitely vanished. The weather was getting worse. It was getting colder and the wind was blowing my fur straight up in the air.

This is no place for a cat, I thought. I am heading for home. Carefully, I picked a safe path through the ice plant and coastal sagebrush and arrived home safely.

James had started a fire in the pot-bellied stove, and I knew my cradle would be nice and cozy. Mr. Featherbee was getting out of his chair as I jumped into my warm bed. I watched him get up and start for the door, and then he stopped abruptly, and looked at James.

He then said, "By cricket, James, I almost forgot. Because you have done a splendid job here for many years, the Commission would like you to stay and live in the lighthouse as a caretaker for as long as you want."

YIPPEE! that was the best news I could hope for. I was very happy.

I wondered if this was part of the BIGGER PLAN the black crow mentioned.

I remember when the black crow told me I shouldn't worry about things I could not control.

He also said that I had a bad CATTITUDE and that I needed to work on my temper and improve my treatment of others.

Now, several years later, I spend my time with James or napping in my cradle. I only pretend to catch mice and the mailman delivers mail to the front door. We are still living in the Lighthouse as Mr. Featherbee promised.

Life is good.

I haven't seen the black crow since Mr. Featherbee was here, but I have a strange feeling the black crow is watching me. I am trying to improve myself, but I have many questions to ask him. I hope he returns someday.

Signed, Jiggs

About the Author

Murray M. Smith was born in 1934, in Ann Arbor, Michigan. He spent his early years on the east side of Detroit. Murray received a BS degree from Michigan State University after serving a tour of duty with the US Marine Corps. With sheepskin in hand he headed west, and in 1967, Mr. Smith founded a consulting engineering company in Sacramento, California. He served as president and CEO until 1992. The Company, now known as "MSA Engineering," celebrated its 50th year reunion in 2017, and is still active today. Murray now resides in Hawaii, on the island of Maui, with his wife Carol of fifty years.

The idea of the book came to Murray while playing golf on the Pacific Grove Golf Course upon learning the story of Jiggs. The mix of a fictional story about a real cat intrigued Murray, and eventually led him to write his first children's book. Murray's search for an illustrator led him to Jonathan Wilson. Jonathan is a recent graduate of the Art College in Hilo, Hawaii, and now resides on Maui. The two of them worked together on a suitable image for Jiggs, in a comedic style. Jonathan's work on the illustrations show a unique talent, which is sure to please the reader. The colorization and artistic touch was added to Jonathon's drawings by Darice McGuire, a local Maui artist, and friend of the Smith's. We hope you enjoy the concerted effort of our team.

CPSIA information can be obtained
at www.ICGtesting.com
Printed in the USA
BVHW022242150720
583810BV00004B/198

* 9 7 8 1 6 4 7 1 8 3 4 6 2 *